I0648902

John O´Connor

Facts about bookworms

Their history in literature and work in libraries

John O´Connor

Facts about bookworms
Their history in literature and work in libraries

ISBN/EAN: 9783337204211

Printed in Europe, USA, Canada, Australia, Japan

Cover: Foto ©Andreas Hilbeck / pixelio.de

More available books at **www.hansebooks.com**

FACTS ABOUT BOOKWORMS

THEIR HISTORY IN LITERATURE
AND WORK IN LIBRARIES

BY
REV. J. F. X. O'CONOR, S. J.

FORMER LIBRARIAN OF FRANCIS XAVIER'S COLLEGE
NEW YORK, GEORGETOWN UNIVERSITY
WASHINGTON, AUTHOR OF "READING
AND THE MIND," "CUNEIFORM IN-
SCRIPTIONS OF NEBUCHADNEZ-
ZAR," ETC.

ILLUSTRATED

NEW YORK : FRANCIS P. HARPER
ONE THOUSAND EIGHT HUN-
DRED AND NINETY-EIGHT : : :

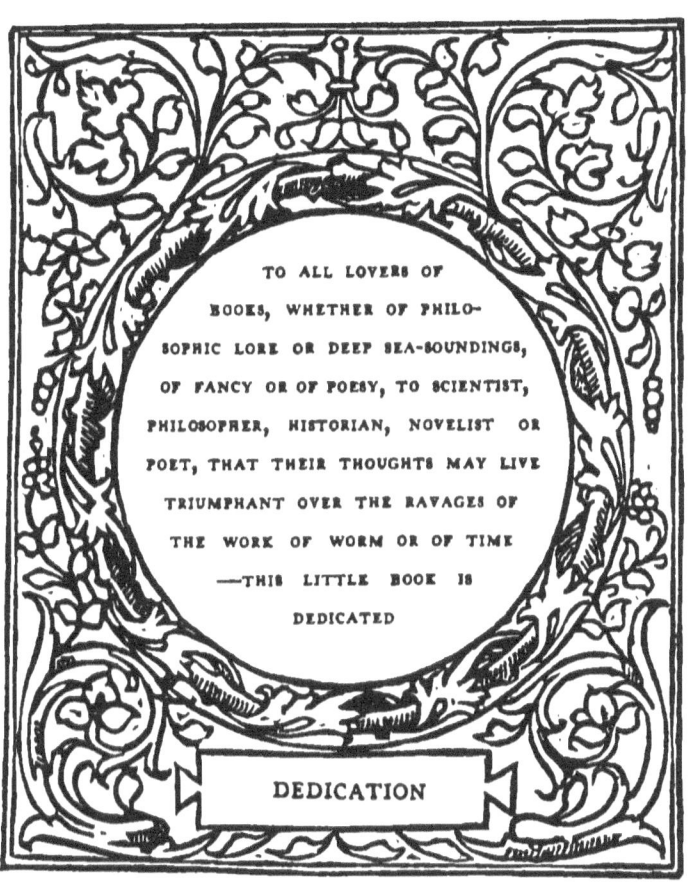

TO ALL LOVERS OF
BOOKS, WHETHER OF PHILO-
SOPHIC LORE OR DEEP SEA-SOUNDINGS,
OF FANCY OR OF POESY, TO SCIENTIST,
PHILOSOPHER, HISTORIAN, NOVELIST OR
POET, THAT THEIR THOUGHTS MAY LIVE
TRIUMPHANT OVER THE RAVAGES OF
THE WORK OF WORM OR OF TIME
—THIS LITTLE BOOK IS
DEDICATED

DEDICATION

PREFACE

1607

THE word "bookworm" suggests to most minds a confused idea. It seems to conjure up a notion that partakes of the world of literature, entomology, history, fiction and humor combined. Is it fact or fiction? Does anyone know? Can they tell us something definite? This was the idea in the mind of the writer before these researches were made. It was the idea in the mind of nearly everyone, as he has found out since by actual experience and questioning on the subject.

To answer these questions: Is the "bookworm" a fact in nature? what is it like? what does it do? what can be told about it?— was the object of these investigations. They are all answered. The research was a slow

Preface

and a patient work, accomplished amid other serious studies.

The interest taken in the question by scholars—literary, historical and scientific—and the appreciation shown, has fully repaid the labor, with the not ungrounded hope that this pioneer work may be followed by further researches that will be for the good and the advantage of letters which have been a gift from God to man in his journey through life.

A strange truth it is, that the same material that supplies food for the spiritual intellect of man should also supply food for one of the tiniest creatures in God's creation.

J. F. X. O'C.

New York,
College of St. Francis Xavier,
January, 1898.

LIST OF ILLUSTRATIONS

                                                FACING PAGE

1. *Facsimile of Aristotle's Descriptions of a Bookworm* . . .   *Title*

2. *A Caxton " Lyfe of our Lady" Eaten by Bookworms. From Blade's " Enemies of Books"* .   *20*

3. *Acarus Cheyletus order Acaridae*   *24*

4. *A Bookworm, from an Engraving of 1665* *35*

5. *Lepisma Saccharina* *39*

6. *A Bookworm found crushed in " Hauy's Mineralogy"* . .   *40*

7. *A copy of "Traité de Mineralogie" from library of Georgetown College, eaten by a Bookworm* *51*

8. *Sitodrepa Panicea* *57*

List of Illustrations

9. *Attagenus Pellio* 58
10. *Ptinus Fur* 63
11. *Dermestes Lardarius* . . . 64
12. *Anthrenus Varius* 69

FACTS ABOUT BOOKWORMS
THEIR HISTORY IN LITERATURE

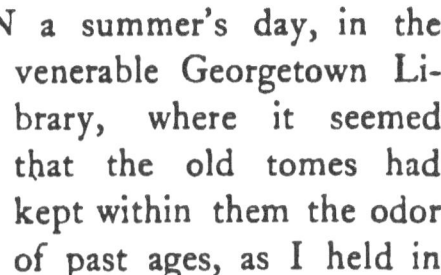N a summer's day, in the venerable Georgetown Library, where it seemed that the old tomes had kept within them the odor of past ages, as I held in my hands an open folio bound in leather, a little ridge of dust along the inner edge of the binding attracted my attention. On closer examination I found small holes near the edge of the dust heaps. Taking a pen-knife I raised the paper on the inside of the cover. When behold! there before me lay a little brown insect. It was cov-

ered with bristles and looked for all the world like a tiny hedgehog, curling himself in his spikes to insure protection. I continued the investigation, and in the same book soon found another, his counterpart. Here was a discovery in truth! "This must be a bookworm," I thought. But how can it be?

The word "bookworm" in my mind was connected with an individual living ever in an atmosphere of letters, dreaming of, and reading perennially, the books that came in his omniverous reach. Had it ever, even in my mind, identified itself with the reality—with the insect world? Never in my imagination had it taken to itself a form whether of bug or of beetle, of moth or of worm that was of any definite shape. Rather it was of the land of myths. Here then was a discovery. I had chanced upon the real, living, visible, palpable creature. A true bookworm visible to the naked eye it was, and it was possible that there were others that might be found under similar conditions. There was a thrill of satisfaction in the thought that I could verify a word that seemed to have hovered on the borderland of fact and of fiction, and to inquiry about which no satisfactory answer had yet been given in the domain of letters. At once the determination framed itself in my mind : " If there is any definite knowledge to be obtained on this subject, that can be secured by no matter what expenditure of patience and time, I am going to take up the question and pursue it to a tangible issue."

Taking my two prizes and placing them securely in a box, I brought them to the President of the University,[1] who was as surprised and interested as myself, and then I began my investigations. With a microscope I studied the movements of my captive strangers. I watched them as, on their backs, they clutched at the empty air with their six small claws, or buried their heads in the paper that I had placed near them to entice them to make use of their mandibles. They were evidently in no humor to do much

[1] The Rev. P. F. Healy, S. J.

boring, as very little was effected during their days of captivity. These two specimens were the Dermestes Lardarius, or larvæ of the brown beetle. At the suggestion of the President of the University I brought them to Mr. Spofford, of the Library of Congress. He sent them to Prof. Baird, of the Smithsonian Institute, and Mr. Baird forwarded them to Mr. Riley, Chief of the Entomological Commission. In the meantime, I continued my researches in this new field of exploration, with no less energy and earnestness than any prospector in his search for gold. Here was something more precious than gold. It was knowledge, a new bit of knowledge—on a small subject, it may be true, but an original addition to the sum total of facts of which the human mind had a firm grasp. No astronomer searching the heavens with his lenses, and feeling a throb of joy as the light of a new star breaks on his vision, felt a keener joy than the knowledge of this new fact brought to me. The new star was but a new number added to millions, here was a

new, unknown, unstudied factor of creation.
Not that it was to upset the established order
of the universe any more than the appearance of a new constellation, but it was the
manifestation of something hitherto imper-
fectly and, it may be said, vaguely known
even until now. I had ever been fond of
books, but never of bugs ; but here was a
bug that was fond of books, and for the
sake of books I could be a friend to the bug
by making his pedigree known to the world
of letters.

But although there was a friendly feeling
for the little creature, was he not an enemy ?
Had not many a precious volume been
made well nigh worthless in supplying him
with his needed repast, and might not better knowledge of him and his trade prevent
the future depredations of his posterity ?
Books are precious things, for in them lies
stored the wisdom of the centuries. The
praise of books is as old as the art of book-
making. From all thinking men the good
book has won not only praise, but venera-

tion. There are, nevertheless, bibliophiles
and bibliophiles. The true lover of books
loves the writer's thought more than the
scriptor's letter, more than the miniatur-
ist's picture or the printer's type. To him
books are the living treasuries of the real
wealth of the centuries. In books he com-
munes with the mightier intellects of the
past—with prophet, philosopher, poet, ora-
tor, historian, with dead heroes and with
dead or dying peoples. The book is a fellow
man, speaking with a voice whose every mod-
ulation the true bibliophile hears far more
clearly than if the phonograph were winding
off the uttered words. The lesser bibliophile
admires books for their rarity, or for the
perfection of some bookmaker's handiwork.
A lover of beauty wholly material, he is
moved by a passion less noble, less pure
than that which controls him who is devoted
only to the soul of the book; and yet
the lesser feeling is not to be despised.
Were it not for its impulses, we should
have been deprived of the enjoyment of

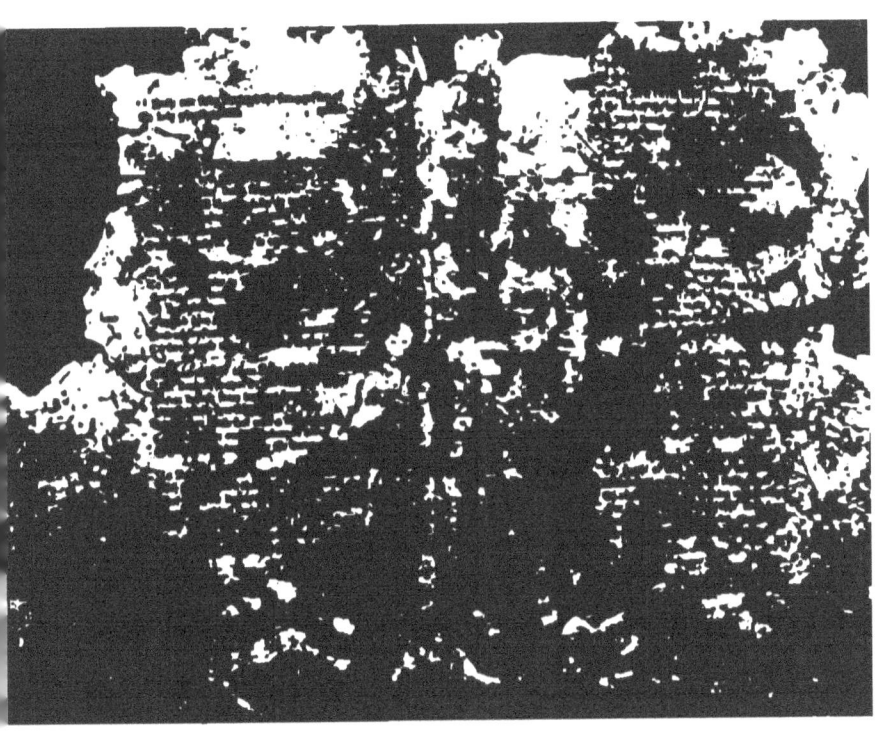

A CAXTON "LYFE OF OUR LADY," EATEN BY BOOKWORMS
FROM BLADE'S "ENEMIES OF BOOKS"

many a " more than golden treasure " of the past.

Though affected by such differing motives, both classes of lovers of books have common interests. Beautiful or unseemly, learned or simple, thoughtful or vain, books run risks that threaten their appearance, their value, or their very existence. In acquiring a knowledge of these risks, and of the best means of protecting the book that is so well loved, the spiritual and material book lover have worked together. They have not, however, exhausted the subject. Therefore it is that one who loves the inside and the outside of good books gladly avails himself of this occasion to "add his mite to the sum of human knowledge," and perhaps by centering the attention of scientific men as well as of the guardians of books on a most destructive enemy, the bookworm, to preserve many a valuable tome to the book lovers of the future.

It is a curious fact that no less a personage than Aristotle has written of the bookworm.

The great philosopher has written: "In old wax, as in wood, there is found an animal which seems to be the smallest of all creatures, called the acarus. It is small and white. And in *books* there are others like those found in cloth, and they are like scorpions without a tail, the smallest of all." These words I quote from a no less ancient and trustworthy authority than Aristotle. The reader will find the original Greek in chapter 32, book V, of the " History of Animals." (See frontispiece.)

Evidently Aristotle knew somewhat about a bookworm, and I am led to believe that he had seen one or more of one possible species. For among the varieties of insects that I have observed in books, there is one, extremely small, hardly visible to the naked eye, pink in color, and corresponding perfectly to Aristotle's description, " like a scorpion without a tail, exceedingly small." In the accompanying cut of *Acarus cheyletus*, the reader will see Aristotle's tailless scorpion, which, by the way, may not be an eater of

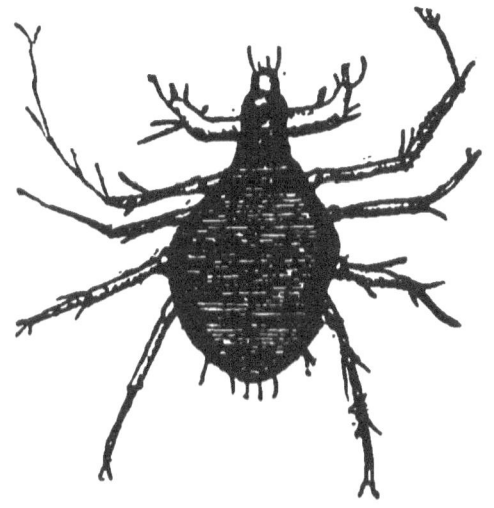

ACARUS CHEYLETUS, ORDER ACARIDÆ
Corresponding to the description by Aristotle, magnified forty times

books. For, though I have found him between the pages, I have never seen him at
work, nor could any of the damage to the
books be reasonably charged to him.

From the great philosopher's mention of
the small creature, " like that found in
cloth," it is fair to infer that in Aristotle's
day the bookworm was eating fine manu-
scripts and making sore even in those days
the heart of the Greek bibliophile. And
since the early days, all through the
Golden Age of Pericles, the worm has been
carrying on its work of destruction. Many
a copy of Aristotle has he eaten full of
holes. The printed book has been spared
no more than the manuscript. One would
imagine that readers of books, curators, book
fanciers, and entomologists, and those who
are often makers of handsome and most use-
ful books, would have spared neither time
nor money in the pursuit of an enemy as
persistent as he is secret. And yet, up to the
present, neither bookmen nor bookmakers
have been able to tell us much more about

the bookworm than Aristotle told twenty-
three centuries ago. In voluminous ency-
clopædias, English or American, there is
scarcely a helpful word. From entomologists one will gather the vaguest and most
imperfect information. Of literary men and
book lovers we shall sum up their knowledge
when we quote Mr. William Blades and Mr.
Andrew Lang. And yet learned societies
have sought to encourage inquiry. Petz-
holdt states that in 1744 the Royal Society
of Science at Göttingen offered a prize for an
answer to these questions : How many kinds
of insects are there inimical to libraries and
archives ? What kind of material do these
insects like best ? What are the best means
of defence against them ? Ninety-eight years
later, in 1842, the Society of Bibliophiles of
Mons offered a prize for a solution of the
same difficulties. To judge from the later
discussions of the subject, these well-meaning
societies did not succeed in securing satisfactory results from the study of the bookworm.

In the " Enemies of Books " Mr. Blades gives a chapter to the bookworm, and there he speaks at greater length of this enemy of books than does any other writer whose works have come under my notice.

" The curious reader," says Mr. Blades, " may wish to be told what this ' bestia audax ' is like. A chameleon-like difficulty at once presents itself. The bookworm offers to us as many varieties of size and shape as there are beholders. According to Sylvester, he is a ' microscopic creature, wriggling on the learned page, which, when discovered, stiffened out into the resemblance of a streak of dirt.' The earliest notice of the bookworm is in ' Micrographia,' by R. Hooke, folio, London, 1665. He calls it ' a small, white, silver shining worm or moth which I found much conversant among books and papers, and is supposed to be that which corrodes and eats holes thro' the leaves and covers. Its head appears big and blunt and its body tapers from it toward the tail smaller and smaller, being shaped almost

like a carrot. . . . The hinder part is ter-
minated with three tails, in every particular re-
sembling the two longer horns that grow out
of the head. The legs are scaled and haired.
This animal probably feeds upon paper and
covers of books and perforates in them small
round holes, finding perhaps a convenient
nourishment in the husks of hemp and flax.'
Hooke's note is interesting. He is not certain that the insect he has seen really feeds
upon books. The 'probably' and 'perhaps'
proved that he has not seen the insect at
work. However, not satisfied with describ-
ing the 'small silver shining worm,' he prints
a drawing or image of the 'booke worm.' "
Mr. Blades reproduces this image, and I have
placed it here that one may the better
appreciate the criticism passed by Mr.
Blades; and that they may also compare
Hooke's image with a real bookworm, to
be noted later, which has been found by me
in books.

"The picture or image," writes Mr.
Blades, "which accompanies the description

is wonderful to behold. Certainly R. Hooke, Fellow of the Royal Society, drew somewhat upon his imagination here, having apparently evolved both engraving and description from his inner consciousness." [1]

Now, if the reader will look carefully at the illustration of the *Lepisma saccharina*,[2] of which I have found three living specimens in books, he will, I am certain, agree with me that R. Hooke did not " evolve both engraving and description from his inner consciousness," but that he made a fairly good drawing of the *Lepisma*. Mr. Blades was hasty in concluding that the drawing given by a member of the Royal Society was altogether a product of his imagination. How slightly entomologists were acquainted with the book-worm Mr. Blades has shown. He quotes Kirby, who identifies it with the larva of *Cranbus pinguinalis*, and others who call it *Aglossa pinguinalis* and *Hypothenemus eruditus*. The Rev. F. T. Havergal, of Cathedral Library, Hereford, says it is a kind of " death watch," with a hard outer skin, dark brown

[1] See p. 34.   [2] See p. 37.

in color, or with white bodies and brown spots on their heads. From other sources we hear of it as *Anobium paniceum, Acarus eruditus, Anobium pertinax*, but we learn little beyond the name and nothing of facts as to its appearance and work. Mr. Blades has seen but three specimens. From what he has been told by librarians and judging by analogy, he "imagined that the following is almost the truth : There are several kinds of caterpillars and grubs which eat into books ; those with legs are the larvæ of moths, those without legs are grubs and turn into beetles." Among the paper-eating species he places three varieties of *Anobium—pertinax, eruditus*, and *paniceum*, of which he gives no proper description, and *Æcophora pseudospretella*, which he calls a moth. "It is," he writes, "about half an inch long, with a horny head and strong jaws."

Mr. Blades' informants were imaginative. A bookworm a half inch long would be a monster. I have seen several, one-twenty-fifth of an inch in length ; several, more than

THE BOOKWORM, FROM AN ENGRAVING OF 1665

From Blades's " Enemies of Books"

one-sixteenth of an inch in length. I have not seen one that exceeded one-eighth of an inch. Mr. Blades gives a photographic illustration of a page eaten by a bookworm. He thinks it "probable" that the guilty worm is the *Æcophora pseudospretella*. The reader may see here an illustration facsimiled from a page from Hauy's Mineralogy in the Georgetown Library.[1] The holes are similar to those shown in the Blades illustration. With my own eyes I have examined the larva of the beetle, the *Ptinus fur*, that has eaten into the Georgetown volume, as he lay dead by the furrows he dug at his last repast. The illustration presents the crushed insect that did the mischief. He was less than one-twenty-fifth of an inch long. A bookbinder once sent Mr. Blades a fat little worm that was found by a workman in an old book. The worm died before reaching maturity. Mr. Waterhouse, of the Entomological Department of the British Museum, examined him before death, and "was of opinion that he was *Æcophora pseudospretella*." Mr. Rye,

[1] See p. 51.

keeper of the printed books in the British Museum, reported that two or three weakly creatures were discovered there in his time. Mr. Adam White, of the Natural History Department, pronounced one of them to be *Anobium pertinax.* In the Bodleian Library Mr. Blades found two worms. One he thoughtlessly threw on the floor and trod under foot. Of the second he was more careful. He boxed it up, intending to study its habits; but, showing it to Dr. Bandinel, the librarian, the doctor promptly crushed the life out of it with his thumb nail.

" Oh, yes, they have black heads sometimes," he said. This one, Mr. Blades assures us, had a white head.

" I never heard of a black-headed bookworm before or since," writes Mr. Blades, and he jocosely suggests that a black-headed variety " in the Bodleian may be accounted for, in consequence of the large number of black-letter books preserved there."

The reader will see opposite this page a black-headed bookworm well known to me.

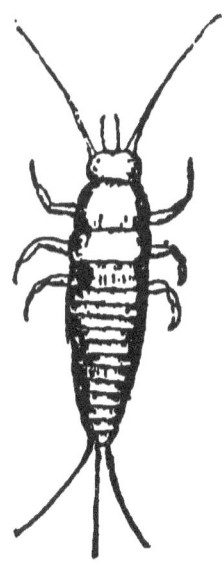

LEPISMA SACCHARINA
Magnified four and a half times

He does not feed on black letter, but on any kind of book he can find.

Mr. Andrew Lang, who has something fresh and bright to say on any and every subject, has a word to say on the black-headed worm in the *Library* (London, 1881) : " In Byzantium the black sort prevailed. Evenus, the grammarian, wrote an epigram against the black bookworm (Anthol. Pal. ix., 251) :

> *' Pest of the muses, devourer of pages, in*
> *crannies that lurkest,*
> *Fruit of the muses to taint, labor of*
> *learning to spoil ;*
> *Wherefore, oh, black-fleshed worm ! Wert*
> *thou born for the evil thou workest ?*
> *Wherefore thine own foul form shapest*
> *thou, with envious toil ? ' "*

And Mr. Lang quotes from " the learned Mentzelius " a bit of amusing information about the bookworm, as he knew it : " Mentzelius says he hath heard the bookworm crow like a cock unto his mate, and ' I knew not,' says he, ' whether some local fowl was clamoring or whether there was but

a beating in mine ears. Even at that mo-
ment, all uncertain as I was, I perceived, on
the paper whereon I was writing, a little insect that ceased not to carol like very chan-
ticleer until, taking a magnifying glass, I as-
siduously observed him. He is about the
bigness of a mite and carries a gray crest,
and the head low-bowed over the bosom ; as
to his crowing noise, it comes of his clashing
his wings against each other with an incessant
din.' What sort of a bird the bookworm
of Mentzelius was I cannot positively say,
but his story of the wondrous crowing re-
minds me of the Rev. F. T. Havergal's
' death watch.'

" If we consult popular natural histories like
that of the Rev. J. S. Wood, we shall find
that 'among the Ptinidæ are placed the little
beetles that eat holes in our furniture, books,'
etc. And knowledge just as indefinite we
may gather from a long line of American,
English, French, German and Italian entomologists. We need not, therefore, be surprised when Mr. Lang tells us that " in our

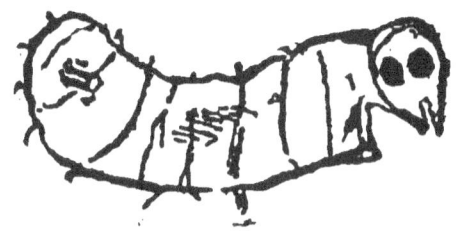

A BOOKWORM FOUND CRUSHED IN THE TREATISE
ON MINERALOGY OF HAUY, MAGNIFIED 40 TIMES

times the learned Mr. Blades, having a desire to exhibit bookworms, in the body, to
the Caxtonians at the Caxton celebration,
could find few men that had so much as seen
a bookworm, much less heard him utter his
wood-notes wild."

The sum of the information, therefore,
that may be derived from writers on the subject of the bookworm, beginning with Aristotle and ending with our contemporaries, is
that there is a bookworm, or that there are
bookworms, with learned names—insects of
some sort, which are suspected of eating books,
though the charge is not proved against any
particular one. Mysteriously they seemed to
have evaded those who were led, or who
should have been led, to determine the spe-
cific nature of bookworms, or to study their
habits. And yet I may be allowed to say
upon positive knowledge that the bookworm
is no rarity, but is a reality, and doing most
decided mischief. Of this it is possible for
me to give full and clear details. As librarian of Georgetown University, of Boston

College, of St. Joseph's College, Philadelphia, and of St. Francis Xavier's College, New York, I have seen and studied a goodly number of bookworms, nor have I confined the inquiries to the libraries under my charge. I have made personal inquiry at Brown University, Providence; at Harvard, at the Boston Athenæum, the Boston Public Library; the Peabody Library, Baltimore; the Congressional Library; and at such great New York libraries as the Astor, the Lenox, and the Mercantile. In the West I have not been, but by correspondence have sought for information but obtained none. It may be there are no worms there. However, there are Dante scholars in the West; and perhaps that true poet, most clever literary man and noted book-lover, the lamented Mr. Eugene Field, might have helped us in tracing the history of the Western worm—not the trichina, but the more deadly bookworm. Since the writer directed the attention of librarians to this subject, specimens have been found in the Lenox and Astor Libraries. And there is but little doubt that examination will prove the disastrous presence of many more.

II

THEIR WORK IN LIBRARIES

TRAITÉ

DE

MINÉRALOGIE,

PAR LE C.n HAÜY,

Membre de l'Institut National des Sciences et Arts, et Conservateur
des Collections minéralogiques de l'École des Mines.

PUBLIÉ PAR LE CONSEIL DES MINES.

En cinq volumes, dont un contient 86 planches.

TOME TROISIEME

DE L'IMPRIMERIE DE DELANCE

PARIS,

CHEZ LOUIS, LIBRAIRE, RUE DE SAVOYE, N.°

(5)

FACTS ABOUT BOOKWORMS
THEIR WORK IN LIBRARIES

MR. BLADES saw only three specimens of what he understood to be bookworms. No other literary man, bibliophile, entomologist or librarian that I know of, and I have consulted many of the prominent librarians of the United States, has claimed to have seen, or has described or pictured a greater number. Mr. Eames, the honored and respected Librarian of Lenox Library, recently found three living insects in a folio on Canon Law, and preserved them as a rare curiosity for those who visited the library. Through his courtesy I examined them and found them to be genuine bookworms with manifest traces of their work, and varying slightly from the larvæ I had previously examined. Multitudes of men have doubted their reality. I have not seen so many as I would have desired for a more complete study, but certainly a larger number than any other record has ever given. Seventy-two specimens of various kinds of insects have I found in books, of such a character as to be classified under the general name of bookworms. A great number of these I found alive and at work eating good books. In the larvæ state I have met them, and in various stages of development, the chief injury being done in the larvæ state. Under a microscope I have seen them, observed them, drawn them. The illustrations of the larvæ that I present are drawn from the actual living, working being. Blades, in the book we have quoted from, appeals to "some patient entomologist to take upon himself to study the habits of this creature, as Sir John Lubbock has those of the ant." Perhaps some men whose calling it is to be patient entomologists will be encouraged by these not impatient studies and researches to continue this work of patient investigation which the leisure moments of other serious studies have but allowed me to begin. " And any man who furnishes reliable information," says Mr. Blades, " if it be only of the ant, as Sir John Lubbock, will be listened to, as Sir John was listened to, and will receive the gratitude of men for his addition to knowledge."

The number of bookworms that I have examined I specify as an argument in favor of the facts here stated. The proportion of three unstudied, as against seventy-two studied specimens, is considerable. In my reading —and I have sought far and wide for facts on the subject—I have found no facts brought forward by any previous author substantiated by study under the microscope and covering a number of specimens of any class. Guesswork, words, fancy, imperfect observation—all these I have found. Perhaps there is no financial result in the pursuit. The

United States Government appropriated a few years ago $28,000 for the investigation of the Rocky Mountain locust and other insects injurious to vegetation; and when I read of the high prices that our American bibliophiles pay for fine manuscript and for early printed books, the classics that I love, the Fathers that I love more, the great men of the Renaissance, our own "Jesuit Relations," the early historians of America, my heart warms to them. Like them, I admire binding, a clasp, old or new, if it be artistic. I am proud to see my fellow countrymen leading, encouraging good workmanship, artistic workmanship, hand-work. In this country I hope to see all the treasures of the past ; and I hope to see American-born men surpass the best that has been done in the printing and in the decoration of good books. Surpass, I say, for I believe that the best in all things is to be done here, in these United States. Here freely, unitedly, intelligently, we can, if we will—and we should—work to surpass the so-called best of all other countries and times—

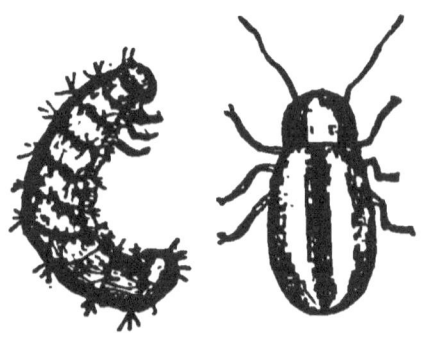

SITODREPA PANICEA

Larva.   Full-grown insect, magnified 11 times

a best that has heretofore controlled, and that now controls us more than enough, and hinders us from doing our best. Still, we cannot do well unless we preserve the past sacredly. Progress, not revolution is our motto. And in books, to make progress, the bookwork-worm must come to a halt.

The bookworm is not a worm, using the word in the scientific sense. It is, in fact, the larva of certain insects belonging to the order of *Coleoptera*, or sheath-winged beetles. In books I have found seven different varieties of larvæ or of full-grown beetles, of which I give the classification as follows :

1. *Sitodrepa panicea*, larva.
2. *Attagenus pellio*, larva.
3. *Sitodrepa panicea*, full-grown insect.
4. *Lepisma saccharina.*
5. *Ptinus fur.*
6. *Dermestes lardarius.*
7. *Anthrenus varius*, larva.

The most voracious of these beetles is the *Sitodrepa panicea*, of which I have examined thirty specimens. Here in New York I have found it, as well as in Washington.   In the larva state it is a soft, white, six-legged " worm " covered with bristles.   It is about one-eighth of an inch long and moves very slowly.   The *Sitodrepa* I have discovered in books ancient and modern, under covers of board, leather and parchment. As a guide to librarians and to bibliophiles, I give a cut of the full-grown beetle as well as of the larva.

The *Attagenus pellio* I have met only once. Long, slender, salmon-colored, with a tail of delicate, wavy hair, it is a most interesting object under the microscope. Looking at it, I could but compare it, in shape. to a miniature whale. In movement the *Attagenus* is most graceful.

Of the full-grown beetle, *Sitodrepa panicea*, I have found, alive and dead, in books old and new, twenty specimens. The insect is very small and brown in color. The *Lepisma saccharina* I have already discussed, when quoting Mr. Hooke and Mr. Blades.

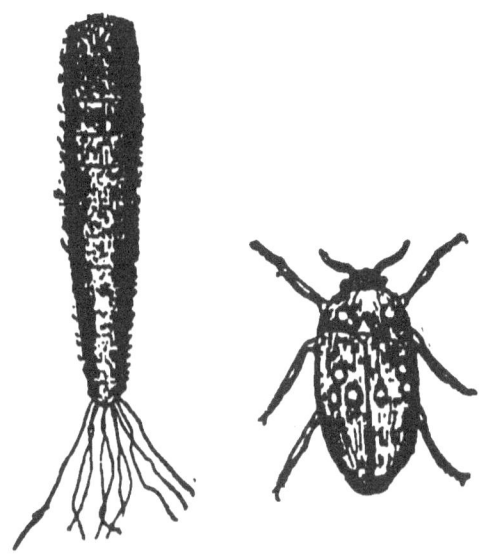

ATTAGENUS PELLIO

Larva, magnified 15 times. Full-grown insect, magnified about 6 times

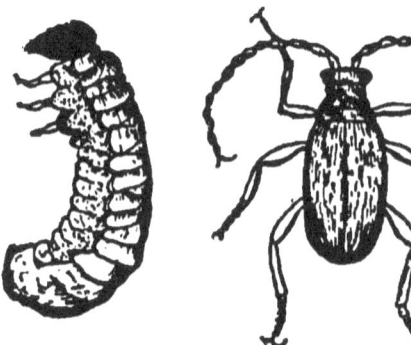

PTINUS FUR

Larva   Full-grown insect

It is cone-shaped, of a silver-gray tint. It has three thick tails. Of the *Lepisma* I have examined four specimens. This insect makes its home in books, but is by no means so destructive as the *Sitodrepa*. The motion of the *Lepisma* is very rapid, like a flash of light.

Ptinus fur—This black-headed worm is found in great numbers and seems willing to eat anything, with due apologies to Mr. Blades and the black-letter text. In appearance the larva resembles the *Sitodrepa*, with the exception of the bristles and shape of the head.

The *Dermestiæ* are well known as consumers of dried animal remains, of plants, and of furs, and many a collector of moths or of butterflies has suffered from the ravages of this little "worm" which will devour anything from a live insect to hard sole leather. In appearance the *Dermestes lardarius* may be compared to a microscopic hedgehog, bristling all over with rough black hairs. Even with a microscope of high power one finds it difficult to determine at which end of the hairy body is the head. Among books this species will be found in great numbers. They leave, especially upon the covers, rougher marks than are made by the other insects here mentioned.

Anthrenus varius—This larva is oval shaped, and varies in form between the almost round *Dermestes* and the elongated *Attagenus pellio*. Like the *Dermestes*, it prefers the bindings of books, while the *Sitodrepa* and *Ptinus* take kindly to the paper.

I have made this description short, as the reader, with plates of drawings from the insects themselves before him, will discern and identify them for himself.

Mr. Blades and others mention other varieties of bookworms. I do not say that the insects they mention are not bookworms, but I have met with none of them. I believe that many of these writers, copying from one another, have adopted names which in some indefinite way have been sanctioned by time. Of the insects referred to by me I have given both description and drawing, with an ac-

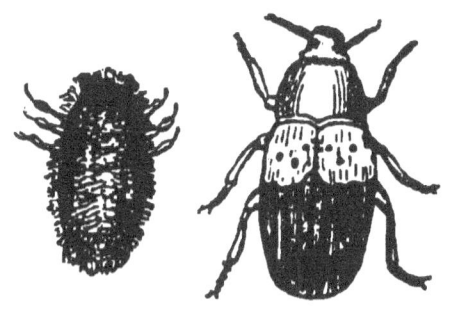

DERMESTES LARDARIUS
Larva, magnified 6 times.   Full-grown insect, magnified 5½ times

ANTHRENUS
VARIUS
Pupa, magnified 13½
times

count of the actual work that has fallen under my personal observation, not once merely, but in many instances. Of the insects referred to by the quoted authors, we have not one illustration, and no definite proof is given of their actual work in books, as usually they were not discovered by the writer who speaks of them, or they have not been carefully examined, consequently the scientific or historical value of references of that kind are of very little importance.

The reader who has not had an opportunity of examining at leisure books in old libraries, can have no idea of the havoc done by these little creatures. With a slight pull I have been able to detach all the binding from the books. The bookworm had eaten away the back. Sometimes the holes cut through the pages are round and regular, and extend in a straight line from cover to cover. Mr. Blades tells the story related by Peignot, and by many men since, of twenty-seven volumes that were pierced in a straight line, presumably by one and the same insect. This reads like a bookworm story. However, we have Piegnot's word for it. Besides, I have five volumes of Hauy's Mineralogy, Paris, 1801, before me now, and scarcely a page of the five volumes is intact. Very often there are deep channels cut into the book, irregular in outline, and these channels will be longer or shorter, and across the width or length of the book. Some pages will be slightly perforated; on others there will be several furrows separated by spaces untouched. Apparently some " worms " have a fanciful appetite. Not infrequently a " worm " burrows deep into a large folio. In a leather-bound folio of Plutarch I found a hole piercing through cover and pages, and in another hole, embedded in the cover, the cocoon of an insect which had not pierced entirely through the cover. In another folio, page after page is pierced. Half-way through the book he ceased work. There is no trace of him. What became of him ? Perhaps some vigorous Dr. Baudinel crushed him under a heavy thumb nail ; perhaps the " worm " had reached a new period of development and returned to the tunnel he had so cleverly constructed, and walked out a full-grown beetle ; or perhaps, again, a greedy *Dermestes* had entered in and made a meal on a " stuffed bookworm," preferring his tender body to the tough vegetable fibre of paper. Even when there is no exterior sign it would be rash to assume that there is not a nest of bookworms in some valued volume. However, the means of detecting the " worm " are simple enough. Inspect closely the back of the bound volume. There you may discover little, smooth, round holes that could have been made with a large needle. Sometimes these holes are at the lower end of the back of the volume ; sometimes they will be found along the edges of the back. Should the back seem to be perfect, then open the book. Between the cover and the fly-leaf you may perceive a little ridge or heap of dust—red, gray or white, according to the color of the binding. If you do perceive such a ridge or heap, the bookworm has been or is in your book. With the point of a knife raise the paper pasted to the cover near the dust heap, and there you will find a *Sitodrepa*, or *Ptinus*, or *Anthrenus*. Clear him out at once ; scrape the book until you are sure there are no unhatched eggs left. " As well kill a man as kill a good book," said Bacon. Better kill the " worm " than let him kill a good book. The bookworm fed on Caxton's, feasts more sumptuously than Cleopatra dreamed of when she drank her dissolved pearl.

No little credit is due to the learned and industrious Mr. Blades for calling attention to this great enemy of our literary treasures. He saw, as others have seen, the great damage done by the bookworm, but he assumed that now this enemy of books was comparatively idle. The worm, Mr. Blades says, will not touch our adulterated modern paper. " His instinct forbids him to eat the China clay, the bleaches, and scores of adulterants now used to mix with the fibre." Thanks, also, " to the general interest taken in old books nowadays, the worm has had hard times of it, and but slight chance of that quiet neglect which is necessary to his existence."

And further on Mr. Blades writes : " Our cousins in the United States, so fortunate in many things, seem very fortunate in this—their books are not attacked by the worm ; at any rate, American writers say so." All our black letter has cost many dollars, and therefore is well looked after, he is sure ; but he is not so certain about our books of the seventeenth and eighteenth centuries, printed in Roman type on wholesome paper. " Probably, therefore," says Mr. Blades, " their custodians of old libraries could tell a different tale." And he is rightly amused because Ringwalt, in his " Encyclopædia of Printing," stated that " there is now in a private library in Philadelphia a book perforated by the insect." " Oh, lucky Philadelphians ! " exclaims the great Caxtonian, " who can boast of possessing the oldest library in the States, but must ask leave of a private collector to see the one worm-hole in the whole city."

Mr. Blades was in error when he claimed
that the bookworm will not touch our adulterated modern paper. Not only in Philadelphia, but in Boston, Providence and New
York, the bookworm eats much modern
paper every year. I have no desire to make
sensational statements, and yet I do not hesi-
tate to say that there is not a large library in
the country which cannot show at least two
wormholes. The Congressional Library has
many books in which there are wormholes.
I have seen them with my own eyes. Were
they eaten before the books came to the
Congressional Library or since ? A little investigation could decide the matter, and the
decision would depend upon how the books
were kept clear of dust and neglect. In the
new Library the books will receive better care.
I have visited the Astor Library, the Cooper
Union, and the Mercantile in New York, and
other libraries in other cities, and I have in-
quired by letter where I have not been person-
ally. There are wormholes in many books in
the Astor Library. In the Cooper Union

there are many perforated volumes. From the answers given to my inquiries one would infer that little harm is done by the book-worm. But because it is not known it does not follow that the damage is not being done, and of this I am able to furnish a striking instance. There is, very, probably, a greater feeling of security than is justifiable. At one of the libraries I visited, the polite curator informed me that, though he was well acquainted with the " biped bookworm," the insect was wholly unknown to him. I asked permission to examine some of the less used volumes, in a duplicate room, and not in old, damp tomes did I look, but into fresh looking volumes of the New York *World* for 1868, and I found several insects hard at work. When I carried the volume and two of the " worms " to the curator he was astonished, as well he might be. On another occasion I surprised the worm at work on bound volumes of the *Scientific American* of the years 1873 and 1875. Prof. Riley, to whom I reported these facts, agreed with me that the claim that only old books were in danger and not recent books of modern paper could not be maintained in face of such testimony. Therefore the theory of Mr. Blades that the bookworm will not eat modern paper vanishes into thin air, but the destructive work continues. It must be admitted as true that the older books run the greater risk, for they are less used. To suppose that insects would injure books in constant use would be absurd. A library of novels is quite safe. No true bookworm would deign to feed on a popular novel. But from the security of new books a librarian may unwisely argue that older and more valuable volumes are untouched. Perhaps, when too late, it will be found that the bookworm has been steadily boring holes through the beautiful pages that had so long stood undisturbed on the shelves. The fact that a librarian has never seen a bookworm does not prove that there are no " worms " fattening on the very choicest morsels in his library. The instance given above is sufficient.

How shall we protect our books against these pests ? When they have once made a lodgment in a book some experts recommend that the book be burned—a heroic if not barbarous measure. I have suggested a thorough scraping and brushing. After this the book should be exposed to sunlight and to air or to gentle heat. Thus the book will be saved. Is there any way by which a large public library may be guarded against their intrusion ? We doubt if there be. Prof. Riley commends pure pyrethrum powder, scattered on the books or shelves, or in books confined in a closed vessel.[1] Camphor has been recommended, as well as fumigation by tobacco, but these are doubtful and somewhat unpractical remedies, as the tightly pressed pages of the book close to the binding, the favorite haunts of the bookworm, are not likely to be reached by fumigation or powder. The bookbinders have been free in suggestion, but if you will consult Mr. Zaehnsdorf, whose book is hardly eleven

[1] See note on p. 87.

years old, and compare him with Mr. Prediger, who wrote just 150 years ago, you will
find that bookbinders' remedies have not
advanced with the centuries. Choose certain
woods for your cases, they say. Poison the
paste, say the bookbinders. They have been
poisoning the paste, and still the bookworm
thrives.[1] Rub the books in March, July and
September with a mixture of powdered alum
and pepper on a piece of woolen cloth, says
Mr. Prediger. Now this rubbing with alum
is very much like the cold-water treatment.
It is not so much the cold water as the treatment that cures. So, it is not the alum that
is important, but the rubbing. Let the
librarian not confine himself to any particular month, but twice or thrice a year let him
overhaul the library, dusting each separate
book, not with a duster but with a cloth.
Wipe, rather than dust. Expensive? Very
well; let a worm eat one expensive volume

---

[1] See note on p. 87. Prof. Riley says: " Use corrosive sublimate." This has been found to be ineffective as it does not seem to
retard the work of the " Bookworm."

and then count the cost. There is no use in trying to hide a patent fact. Some shelves even in the best-managed libraries are permitted to receive and retain a layer of dust; and where there is dust, poor ventilation, and lack of light, sooner or later the bookworm will enter in and devour. The eggs of the insects are deposited with the dust. Under favorable conditions of quiet, heat, bad air, the eggs are hatched, the bookworm is alive and hungry, and the work of ruin begins. Where will it end? When will it be discovered? Oftentimes only too late, when some great literary treasure of priceless value has been utterly ruined.

The facts about bookworms are these. There are bookworms, the real living insects. They are not a thing of the past but are doing mischief to-day. They eat not only old books, but all books; not only vegetable fibre paper but any kind of paper. They are not known. They revel in libraries. They destroy there, where they are not suspected, where the suggestion of their presence would be scoffed at. In some cases the mischief has been irreparable and will be so in more than one future case.

Another fact is that more care should be taken of books in public and private libraries.

In conclusion, it is to be hoped that the present volume may furnish to all readers a solution to the doubt whether there is a real bookworm ; furthermore, that it may give to those who may have so desired a definite idea of the work and habits of this enemy of letters. The gathering of these results has taken years of patient toil, and it is with the hope that some patient entomologist or librarian may perfect the investigations here set on a footing that these researches are made known to the literary and scientific world.

APPENDIX

ENTOMOLOGICAL NOTES

APPENDIX

ENTOMOLOGICAL NOTES

Spencer F. Baird, Commissioner.

UNITED STATES COMMISSION,
FISH AND FISHERIES.

Washington, D. C., April 4, 1881.

Dear Sir :

On receiving specimens referred to by Fr. O'Conor I transmitted it with the accompanying communications to Prof. Riley, and now beg to enclose herewith his reply, together with the letter of Fr. O'Conor.   Yours truly,

(Signed)   Spencer F. Baird.

A. R. Spofford, Esq.,
    Librarian of Congress,
            Washington.

Enclosure.

Facts about Bookworms

LIBRARIAN OF CONGRESS,
COPYRIGHT OFFICE
UNITED STATES OF AMERICA.
Library of Congress,
Washington, April 5, 1881.

Dear Sir :

I have received the enclosed from Prof. Baird regarding the insects referred to him. The article in the Entomologist referred to has the same remedies to recommend (with one exception) which Prof. Riley notes in his letter. Very respectfully,   (Signed)   A. R. Spofford,
                                        Librarian Congress.
Rev. J. F. X. O'Conor, S. J.,
    Georgetown College.

DEPARTMENT OF AGRICULTURE,

DIVISION OF ENTOMOLOGY.

Washington, D. C.   , 188

Reference to descriptions and illustrations of insects injurious to libraries :

Ptinus fur Linn—Sometimes very common in old books, the larvæ boring galleries through paper covers and often through large volumes. The beetle has often been figured, the best being in Sturm's *Insecten Deutschland's* vol. XXI. A very good description of larva aud pupa is given by De Geer, *Memoires pour servir a l'histoire des insects*, 1753, vol. IV (plate IX).

Ptinus dubius Dufts—Beetle figured, with an account of its injuries to books in *American Entomologist*, vol. II, pp. 32–33. The larva has never been described or figured.

Sitodrepa panicea. The most common library pest. An

account, with figure of the beetle, is in *American Entomologist*, vol. II, pp. 32–33. The larva has been described and figured by Frisch, *Beschreibungen von allerlei Insecten Deutschland's*, 1721, vol. II, pp. 36-38, tab. 8, figs. 1-3. Frisch's description has often been copied by later authors but there is no other figure of the larva.

Dermestes lardarius Linn—This and the two following chiefly feed on dry animal matter, *e. g.* leather, the larvæ being unable to bore galleries through paper. Beetle and larva often described and figured, the most accesible being in C. V. Riley's *VI The Report on the Insects of Missouri*, fig. 27 and in *American Entomologist*, vol. II, p. 308.

Attagenus megatoma—Beetle and larva figured in Sturm's *Insecten Deutschland's*, 1847, vol. XIX, tab. 354.

Attagenus pelleo—Larva figured by Chapuis & Candeye, *Catalogue des larves des Coleoptères* (in Memoires de la Sociéte Royale des Sciences de Liège, 1853.) tab. 3, fig. 3. A good desciption of beetle and larva is by Erichson, *Naturgeschichts der Insecten Deutschland's*, vol. III, pp. 438–439.

Hypothenemus eruditus Westwood—Larva and beetle boring in wooden covers. Larva never described but common in dry twigs of various trees. Beetle described and figured by Westwood in Transactions London Entomology Society, vol. I, p. 34, tab. 7, fig. 1 a-g. Beetle also described under the name of *Hypothenemus hispidedus*, by Dr. Lelonte in Transactions Amer. Entom. Society, 1868, p. 156.

Celetus eruditus, Psocus domesticus, amabilis, geologus— I can only refer to American Entomologist, vol. II, p. 324, where *Termes* is mentioned ; for *Lepisma domestica* and *sac-*

Facts about Bookworms

charina to Packard's Guide to the Study of Insects, 3d ed.,
pp. 622-623.

C. V. RILEY, Chief,   HEADQUARTERS,
    Washington, D. C.

A. S. PACKARD, JR., Sec'y.   No. 1700 13th St., N. W.,
    Providence, R. I.

CYRUS THOMAS,   Washington, D. C.
    Disbursing Agent,
        Carbondale, Ill.

DEPARTMENT OF THE INTERIOR,
OFFICE OF THE
U. S. ENTOMOLOGICAL COMMISSION,
Washington, D. C., April 1st, 1881.

DEAR PROF. BAIRD—

Yours with enclosures from Mr. Spofford and from Mr.
J. F. O'Conor, of Georgetown College, are to hand and
contents noted. I find in the box only three of the insects
specifically referred to by Mr. O'Conor as injuring books,
the fourth is missing and may be one of the many insects
known to do injuries to libraries. The first which he refers
to is an immature larva of a species of *Dermestes* and probably of the common *D. lardarius*; the second insect referred
to is the larva of the third, which is also one of the worst
and commonest enemies of books, and is known to entomologists as *Sitodrepa panicea*. This beetle not only at-
tacks books in the larva state, but all other kinds of preserved material. It is found in almost all kinds of drugs,
and is one of the worst enemies the druggist has to contend

86

Entomological Notes

with. It infests also wheat and other stored grain, and I have known it to injure seriously show stock by boring through the leather, and have suffered from its work in my own collection of insects. Sheep-bound books seem to be preferred by this insect, cloth-bound books being less often injured. One of the best ways of ridding books of this, as well as other pests, is to subject the volumes to a considerable heat in the baking oven, being careful, however, not to burn the leather brittle. It would be even better to place them in a water-tight box and then to sink them into hot water. Though it has not been tried yet, I have faith that pure *Pyrethrum* powder scattered among the books in a closed vessel would also effectually free them. The only way to actually prevent the attack of these pests is to use corrosive sublimate in the binder's paste. I would refer you, finally, for further particulars as to these and other book pests to an article published in 1870 in the *American Entomologist*, vol. II, p. 322.

Yours very truly,

(Signed) C. V. RILEY.

PROF. SPENCER F. BAIRD,
  Secretary Smithsonian Institution,
  WASHINGTON, D. C.

THE END

www.ingramcontent.com/pod-product-compliance
Lightning Source LLC
Chambersburg PA
CBHW032355020726
47499CB00008B/2764